AR(R) 3.4 MG
P+S. 1.0
#145398

COWBOY UP

BY JAKE MADDOX

TEXT BY
SCOTT WELVAERT

ILLUSTRATIONS BY
SEAN TIFFANY

STONE ARCH BOOKS
a capstone imprint

Jake Maddox books are published by Stone Arch Books
A Capstone Imprint
151 Good Counsel Drive, P.O. Box 669
Mankato, Minnesota 56002
www.capstonepub.com

Library of Congress Cataloging-in-Publication Data
Maddox, Jake.
  Cowboy up / by Jake Maddox ; text by Scott R. Welvaert ; illustrated by Sean Tiffany.
     p. cm. -- (Jake Maddox sports story)
  Summary: Jake is the best bull rider in his division, but after he finally takes a bad spill during a competition he has to overcome his fear before he can ride again.
  ISBN-13: 978-1-4342-2989-2 (library binding)
  ISBN-10: 1-4342-2989-0 (library binding)
  ISBN-13: 978-1-4342-3425-4 (pbk.)
  ISBN-10: 1-4342-3425-8 (pbk.)
  [1. Bull riding--Fiction. 2. Self-confidence--Fiction. 3. Fear--Fiction.] I. Welvaert, Scott R. II. Tiffany, Sean, ill. III. Title.
  PZ7.M25643Co 2011
  [Fic]--dc22
                                        2011000346

Art Director: Kay Fraser
Graphic Designer: Russell Griesmer
Production Specialist: Michelle Biedscheid

Photo Credits: Shutterstock/Photography Perspectives - Jeff Smith (cover)

Printed in the United States of America in Stevens Point, Wisconsin.
082011
006341R

EC
mad

BC 20526

$19.89

12/11 Garrett Book Co.

TABLE OF CONTENTS

CHAPTER 1
THE TOUGHEST BULL IN THE DIVISION

Jake Monson took a seat on a bench in the arena prep station. He reached down and pulled on his cowboy boots. The announcer's voice echoed throughout the arena. In the stands, people cheered. Jake's turn to ride was coming up soon.

I hope I get a strong bull in the draw, he thought. He was already in the finals, but Jake wanted to win it all. The only way to do that was to ride a high-ranking bull.

"Did you watch me, Jake?" asked his friend Alicia. She sat down next to him, took off her leather gloves, and tossed her safety helmet aside. She put her cowboy hat on instead. She had just finished her final run. Now she could watch the others.

"Of course," Jake said. "Blue Stinger is a tough bull to ride. You stayed on him all eight seconds. Your score will be awesome."

Their friend Brandon ran down the arena ramp and into the prep station. "You guys have to see this!" he yelled. "Kyle's doing it!"

"Doing what?" Alicia asked.

Brandon smiled. "Riding King Minos," he said. "He's trying to make it into the semi-finals. His only chance is to ride the toughest bull here."

The three of them ran up the ramp to get a better view. Soon, they were in the stands next to the bucking chute. Inside the chute, Kyle sat on an enormous bull. That was King Minos. The bull's snort echoed so loudly that it hushed the crowd. He sounded like a dinosaur.

King Minos had never let any rider last eight seconds. Most riders didn't even last four. It would take talent to stay on for the full time. Anyone who did it would be known as the best.

Jake knew all of these things. He was the best rider in his division and the reigning champion. No bull had ever thrown him. He had a perfect record.

A buzzer rang through the arena. The gate swung open.

King Minos exploded out of the chute. He violently bucked three times. Each time, Kyle's body whipped up and down. King Minos whirled and spun.

Kyle managed to stay on, but he tilted to one side. The last series of spins and kicks had nearly unseated him. Jake could see Kyle's hand slipping off of the bull rope. He was barely holding on. Then King Minos pulled out a violent spin, twist, and kick combo.

Kyle flew high into the air and crashed to the dirt in the arena. Rodeo clowns quickly ran out to round up King Minos. The ride was finished. It had only lasted three seconds. Kyle wouldn't make the final cut.

"Jeez," Alicia muttered.

Brandon shook his head. "I know," he agreed. "Riding that bull is beyond crazy. I can't believe he even tried that. No rider has ever lasted eight seconds on that monster."

"Not yet, anyway," Jake muttered under his breath.

Alicia and Brandon looked at him. "What does that mean?" Alicia asked.

"I'm hoping I draw King Minos," Jake said to his friends. "I think I can take him. No problem."

Brandon shook his head. "Your score is already good enough to make it to the finals, Jake," he said. "What's the point of riding King Minos? You should just hope for a low-ranked bull and coast into the finals."

"Brandon's right," Alicia said. "What if you get thrown? Or what if you're hurt? If something happens, you might not be able to ride in the finals."

"I don't want to just make the finals," Jake said. "I want to win. Besides, I've never been thrown by any bull." He shrugged. "That's not going to change now."

CHAPTER 2
AN UNSTOPPABLE FORCE

A few minutes later, Jake got his wish. He drew King Minos for his last round. Alicia and Brandon were shocked as Jake headed into the arena.

"Wait!" shouted Alicia. She and Brandon followed Jake down the corridor. "You don't have to ride. Your first score was good enough!"

Jake kept walking. "I drew King Minos," he said. "I'm not backing down."

Alicia and Brandon caught up to him. Brandon grabbed Jake's arm from behind. "You're just showing off," Brandon said. "Your first run was practically perfect. Don't risk it."

"This is dangerous," Alicia added. "Don't be stupid."

"It's only eight seconds," Jake said. He climbed the railing to the bucking chute. "Trust me. I know what I'm doing."

Brandon sighed and shook his head. He nudged Alicia. "Come on," he said. "We're not going to change his mind. Let's get to the stands."

From the rail, Jake watched the handlers try to guide King Minos into the bucking chute. It took four men to get the bull to the entrance of the chute.

Before entering, Minos shook his head violently. The bull kicked its rear legs at the handler behind him and snorted loudly as the handlers pushed him forward.

Jake looked down at the bull below him. *It's just eight seconds, right?* he thought. *No big deal.* But for the first time, he felt nervous.

Jake took a deep breath and lowered himself onto King Minos. He checked the tape on his leather gloves. Then he grabbed the bull rope and made sure it fit tightly in his right hand.

Fans cheered, filling the small arena with noise. Across the arena, his family was watching. Alicia and Brandon had found seats next to them. Jake smiled and nodded in their direction.

Jake took another deep breath. He felt King Minos trembling beneath him. The bull's muscles were tense and vibrating with energy.

The arena buzzer blared in his ears. At the front of the bucking chute, the gate swung open. Show time.

King Minos leaped out of the chute, kicking up a cloud of dirt behind him. In that first, long second, the bull spun twice, kicking violently after each spin. Jake tightened his grip and tried to let his body react to the bull's movements.

The next couple of seconds were a blur. Jake's head snapped up and down as the bull leaped and kicked. The arena spun around him. Everything seemed to blend together.

King Minos suddenly bucked and kicked his way to the wall. Jake saw the wall coming just before he smashed into it. Dazed, he held on.

Three seconds left, Jake thought.

But King Minos had other plans. The huge bull bucked and kicked his way back into the center of the arena. Jake felt his grip slipping. His legs lost contact with the bull. With another giant kick, King Minos threw Jake off.

Even though Jake's body was thrown from the bull, his right hand got caught in the bull rope. As he landed, he heard it — a pop from his right shoulder.

Jake tried to untangle his hand. But King Minos dragged him for three whole seconds before he fell loose.

Jake lay crumpled on the ground, his arm on fire with pain. He managed to look up at the arena stop clock to check his time.

Seven seconds.

He'd missed it by one second.

CHAPTER 3

EIGHT WEEKS

Jake sat upright in his hospital bed, a pile of pillows propped behind him. He had bandages wrapped around his right shoulder. A heavy sling cradled his right arm. His dad sat in a chair next to the bed.

"I dislocated my shoulder," Jake said when Brandon and Alicia walked into the room. "They had to go in and repair some ligaments or something. I have six stitches. Want to see?"

Jake's dad shook his head. "The doctor said to keep the bandages on for now," he said.

"What about the finals?" Alicia asked.

Jake looked down. "The doctor said I can't use my arm," he answered.

"For how long?" Brandon asked.

"Eight weeks," Jake said. "I have to let my shoulder heal for eight weeks."

Alicia smiled. "Finals are in ten weeks!" she said. "That means you'll be healed in time to compete. Right?"

Jake's father shook his head. "I don't know, kids," he said. "Jake's shoulder might be healed in eight weeks, but his arm will still be weak. I don't think he'll make the finals. But there's always next year."

"Yeah," Jake said, sighing. "Next year, I guess."

Alicia said, "Well, get better. We'll see what happens."

Brandon shook his head. "One more second, and you would have had it, man!" he said. "That was still really good, though."

"Thanks," Jake said.

After Brandon and Alicia left, Jake lay in bed thinking. *They warned me about this,* he thought miserably. *Why didn't I listen to them?*

Jake shook his head. Images of the huge bull flashed in his mind. The bucking. The spinning. The pop of his shoulder. The pain. He couldn't shake the memory from his thoughts.

"Don't worry, Jake," Dad said. "We'll get you all healed up, and next year you'll be better than ever!"

"Yeah, right," Jake mumbled. "Better than ever."

CHAPTER 4
LEFT-HANDED CHORES

Four weeks later, Jake was more discouraged than ever. He felt like he couldn't do anything.

He tried helping out his father on the ranch. Mucking the horse stalls really didn't go well. The rake wouldn't go where he wanted. Plus, the actual raking part didn't work. He didn't have the strength to press down and pull the muck out of the stall with just his left hand.

Jake threw the rake to the ground in frustration.

He decided to try feeding the horses. He went to the feed room and managed to fill a bucket with oats. But when he got to the stall, he realized he had a problem. His good hand was holding the handle.

Great. How am I supposed to tip the bucket? Jakes thought. He leaned over and lifted his knee to tip the bucket. The oats spilled all over the floor.

Angry, Jake threw the empty bucket on the ground and stomped out of the barn.

Outside, Jake's father watched as he kicked a clump of dirt. Dad took off his gloves and walked over. "Why don't you help me with this fence rail?" Dad suggested.

"Fine," said Jake.

His dad lifted the fence rail into place. "Hold this up for me," he said. Jake lifted the rail and held it while his father drilled the hole.

"I know how you feel," Dad said.

"What do you mean?" Jake asked. He doubted his dad knew how frustrated and scared he was feeling.

"You had a fall," his father said. "It happens to everyone. But you'll be okay. Your arm will heal. And then next season, you'll get back on that bull, and everything will be fine."

Jake thought about his fall. "I don't know, Dad," he said quietly. "I don't know if I can do it again. I keep seeing that bull in my head."

His dad stopped drilling and looked at him. "I know you're scared," he said. "You hurt more than your arm when you fell. But the important thing is that you need to cowboy up and get back to doing what you do best."

"What does 'cowboy up' mean?" Jake asked.

"It means overcome your fears," Dad said. "Dust yourself off and get back on the bull."

Images of King Minos flashed in Jake's mind again. He felt his heart racing, and his palms got sweaty.

When he let go of the rail, Jake noticed that his good hand shook with fear. To make it go away, he clenched his hand into a fist.

He shook his head. *Get a grip*, he told himself.

Just then, he heard a voice calling his name. "Jake!"

Jake turned. Alicia and Brandon were coming across the yard toward him. Both wore their riding gear and carried practice helmets.

"We needed to see old 'One-Arm' Jake," Brandon said. "If your dad is okay with it, we'd like to take a few rides on Hot Streak. Your dad's bull is always good for a practice run."

Jake glanced over at his dad to make sure it was okay. Dad nodded.

"You bet," Jake said. Together, the three of them walked around to the bullpen out back where his dad kept Hot Streak.

Behind the barn, Jake helped Brandon and Alicia get Hot Streak ready. Brandon climbed up onto the bull's back. When the gate swung opened, the pair shot into the bullpen.

Jake watched as Brandon rode Hot Streak around the practice ring. Brandon held on to the bull rope with his right hand. His left hand was held high in the air as Hot Streak spun, twisted, and bucked. After seventeen long seconds, Brandon finally fell off.

"Good run, Brandon," Jake said.

"My turn," Alicia said.

On her ride, Alicia held the bull rope in her left hand. As Hot Streak twisted and kicked, Alicia stayed on the bull. Her right arm waved above her head like a ribbon.

That's weird, Jake thought. *I never realized she was left-handed.*

Jake looked down at his right arm in the sling. Then he looked at his good left arm.

"I think I have an idea," Jake said.

CHAPTER 5
BACK ON THE BULL

Jake was back at the doctor's office four weeks later. He'd just gotten his sling taken off.

"Your arm is still going to be pretty weak, Jake," the doctor said as he looked at Jake's arm. The doctor was doing one last check to make sure his arm was healing. "I want you to try to take it easy, okay?" he said. "Be careful with it."

"Okay," Jake said.

* * *

Soon, Jake's arm started to feel better. He felt stronger each day. After a few days, he could muck the horse stalls and dump oats in the trough without spilling them.

By the time his sling had been off for a week, things were going pretty well. It was time to try to ride again.

"Jake?" Alicia called from the doorway of the barn. "Are you ready to go?"

Jake hung up the feed bucket. "You bet!" he called back.

Behind the barn, Brandon sat on top of the bucking chute rail. Hot Streak rattled in the bucking chute, eager to get out.

"He's really wound up, Jake," said Brandon. "You sure you're ready for this?"

Jake rubbed his shoulder. *Am I ready for this?* he wondered. *Maybe I should wait. What if I fall off again?*

Jake thought back to his last ride on King Minos. The fiery eyes. The pounding of the bull's hooves. He felt his heart race again. The sweaty palms came back.

"Time to cowboy up," Jake muttered under his breath. He taped his gloves tightly around his wrists. Then he checked his boots and spurs. Everything looked good. Jake used his strong left arm to climb up the rail.

Brandon handed him a safety helmet. "If you're going to fall, make sure you fall on your good shoulder," he said.

"What good would that do?" asked Jake. "Then I'd have two bad shoulders."

"Good point," Brandon admitted. "Maybe you should try not to fall, period."

Jake climbed on top of the bull and tucked his left hand under the bull rope. He gripped the rope as tightly as he could.

It felt different holding the rope with his left hand. Everything seemed backward. *Here goes nothing*, Jake thought. He looked up at Brandon and nodded. Brandon opened the chute.

Hot Streak shot out into bullpen. Jake held on tight with his left hand, but his rhythm and all his movements felt off. He had to think backward. The bull spun and bucked hard. Jake fell off into the mud after just one second.

"Wow," Alicia said. "You're not a very good lefty, are you?"

Jake didn't answer. His hands were starting to shake. Just looking at Hot Streak made him think of King Minos.

I have to get a grip and cowboy up, Jake thought. "Again," he said.

Alicia hopped down from the fence and wrangled up Hot Streak. Brandon set the chute for the next run. Then Jake climbed on board for a second try.

Brandon glanced at Jake to make sure he was ready to go. Jake nodded, and Brandon opened the chute. Hot Streak flew out.

This time, Jake made sure to think backward. He gripped the bull rope tightly in his left hand and let his body flow with the bull. For every kick, buck, and spin, Jake reversed his thinking.

He lasted three whole seconds before Hot Streak tossed him into the mud. His heart was racing, but he didn't feel panicked. No signs of King Minos anywhere.

"Again!" Jake said, picking himself back up.

He tried again. This time, he lasted five seconds before being bucked into the mud. His clothes were dirty, and mud caked his helmet.

"Again," he yelled.

On his fourth try, Jake held on for seven seconds. He picked himself up out of the mud again and walked over to the bucking chute. All of his muscles were sore. Alicia and Brandon were waiting for him.

"It's kind of different doing it left-handed, isn't it?" asked Alicia.

"Yeah," Jake said. "But I think I'm getting it."

"Again?" asked Brandon.

Jake looked at his friend. "Oh, yeah," he said.

CHAPTER 6
THE FINALS!

A week later, Jake sat in the first row of the Galveston Arena with his parents and sister. It had been three weeks since he'd gotten his sling off. He flexed his fingers and bent his elbow to loosen up. The muscles were still weak.

"Hey, Jake!" yelled Alicia from the bucking chute. "Just because you're recovering from that spill doesn't mean I'll go easy on you. I'm here to win!"

The arena buzzer sounded, and the gate swung open. Alicia and her bull flew out. She rode well and lasted the full eight seconds. Her score put her in first place.

After her ride, Alicia sat with Jake. Brandon was up next. "Are you going to go left-handed or right?" Alicia asked as Brandon got ready to ride.

Jake rotated his right arm to test his shoulder. It didn't hurt, but it still felt weak. "I think I'd better stay with the left," he said.

In the arena, Brandon rode a high-ranked bull for the full eight seconds. It wasn't his best ride, but his score still put him in the top five.

Brandon joined them after his run. "What's your plan, Jake?" he asked. "Who are you riding?"

"Razorwire," Jake said, glancing over at his friend.

Jake thought about the bull he'd drawn. Razorwire was a mid-ranked bull. He'd make for a good comeback challenge. But all Jake could think about was King Minos. *I have to cowboy up*, he thought.

"That's a good bull," Brandon said. "Tommy Maskin rode him earlier. Got tossed in six seconds. But I'm sure you'll last longer."

Jake glanced up at the arena. The stands were packed.

"Don't worry about the crowd," Brandon told him. "You'll be fine. Just get back out there on that bull." He walked with Jake to the bucking chute to prepare for his first run.

Brandon helped Jake check his helmet, gloves, and boots. Then Jake climbed the rail and lowered himself onto Razorwire. He gripped the bull rope securely in his left hand. Jake could feel the bull tense underneath him. An image of King Minos flashed into his head.

I can't think about that now, Jake told himself. *I have to concentrate.*

The arena buzzer blared, and the chute opened. Razorwire came out of the chute spinning.

Razorwire spun into a series of jumps and kicks. The bull kicked its way closer to the wall. Jake remembered how much it had hurt when he crashed into the wall last time. Razorwire spun, kicking the wall hard with his back legs.

Jake slid backward on the bull. The kick off the wall had knocked him loose. He had to hold on tighter. He knew what the bull would do next.

Razorwire leaped into the air and kicked hard. All at once, Jake lost his grip on the bull rope. He flew off the bull and hit the arena dirt hard.

Rolling over, he looked up at the clock. Five seconds.

CHAPTER 7
BAD LUCK

At the end of the first round, Alicia was in first place and Brandon was in fifth. Jake wasn't even on the board.

During Brandon's final ride, Jake sat in the first row of the crowded arena.

Brandon had drawn a mid-ranked bull named El Dorado for his final ride. As Jake watched, Brandon settled onto the back of the bull. Then the buzzer rang, and the chute flew open.

El Dorado came out fired up. Right away he went into three powerful kicks and a long spin. Jake thought Brandon was done for, but somehow he managed to hold on.

Then El Dorado launched into a tight set of spins. Brandon held his arm high and held on. He only had three seconds left. El Dorado continued to kick his way around the arena. There were a few times Jake thought Brandon would slip, but he didn't.

Jake looked up at the clock. Eight seconds. The buzzer rang again, and Brandon quickly jumped off the bull.

The ride was good enough to move Brandon into first place. Jake cheered as his friend walked up the ramp to the front row seats. "Did you see my ride?" Brandon asked.

"Yeah," Jake said. "That was your best ride yet!"

Brandon sat down next to him and pulled the tape off of his gloves. "Who'd you draw for your next ride?" he asked.

"I don't know," Jake said. "I've been watching the scoreboard to see. I just hope it's not Minos."

"Don't be ridiculous," Brandon said. "There's no way you'll draw the same bull that knocked you out nine weeks ago."

"Come on," Jake said. "Don't jinx me!"

They both watched the scoreboard as the next batch of draws were made. One by one, names of bulls appeared next to riders. As the name of his bull slid onto the board, Jake's heart pounded.

King Minos.

Jake felt his heartbeat speed up. His palms grew sweaty. He remembered the pain of his shoulder popping.

I don't think I can do this, Jake thought frantically. Sure, he'd worked hard to recover and get back in the finals — but not for this bull.

I need some air, he thought. Jake got up from his seat and walked out of the arena.

Out by the concession stand, Jake sat on the floor by the condiment table. He wore his cowboy hat low over his face. His father walked up to the stand and bought two hot dogs. Then he walked over to the condiment table and piled one hot dog with relish.

"Lots of mustard on yours, right?" Dad asked Jake.

Jake looked up. "I can't eat a hot dog before a ride, Dad," he said. "I'll throw up all over the bull."

"Are you going to ride?" his dad asked.

Jake looked down again. "I don't know," he said.

Dad sat down next to him. "I know you think it's impossible, Jake," he said. "I've been in the same situation. Are you getting sweaty palms?"

"Yeah," Jake said.

"Is your heart racing?" his dad asked.

"Yes," Jake admitted.

"And I bet that bull keeps thundering through your mind, right?" Dad asked.

"Exactly," Jake said, nodding. "How'd you know?

Dad smiled. "I used to ride too, you know," he said. "When I was sixteen, a bull named Peachie threw me off. I broke my leg."

"The bull was named Peachie?" Jake asked, laughing.

"Yes," his father said. "You think you have it tough? At least your bull's got a good name." Dad shook his head. "The point is, the year after my busted leg, I won it all."

"Yeah, I know," Jake said. "You rode every day of the week for a whole year. You practiced. You worked hard."

"That wasn't all I did," his dad said. "You think I wasn't scared to get back on? Of course I was. But I couldn't let that stop me from doing something I loved."

"So how did you get over it?" Jake asked.

"I had to cowboy up," his dad said. "Just like you. You can't overcome your fears without taking them by the horns. You get it?"

Jake looked up his dad. "Yeah," he said with a smile. "I get it."

CHAPTER 8
RETURN OF THE KING

Jake and his dad headed back into the arena. It was time for Alicia's final run. She'd drawn a mid-ranked bull named Warclub, a chocolate-colored bull with huge horns.

Alicia held onto the bull rope with her left hand. Her right hand waved as her body lurched with the bull. She made it through the eight seconds. The crowd went wild.

Jake thought about what he needed to do for his final run. His first run had not been good. He'd have to ride Minos perfectly to move into the top ten.

Jake gulped. His throat was dry, and he could barely swallow. Visions of King Minos raced through his mind.

Jake shook his head. He knew he couldn't let King Minos get to him. *Come on, cowboy up*, he told himself.

"Wake up," said Alicia, sitting down next to him. "Did you see my score?"

Jake glanced at the scoreboard. Alicia was in first place again. Brandon had been bumped to third. "Wow," Jake said. "You might be the new champion."

"If you have a perfect ride on King Minos, maybe not," Alicia said.

"Don't count on it," Jake muttered, rubbing his face. "I couldn't ride him nine weeks ago, and that was when both of my arms worked."

"Just do your best," Alicia said. "Everyone here is rooting for you."

"Come on, Jake," Brandon called. He stood near the bucking shoot. "Your turn."

Jake took a deep breath and stood up. "Time to go," he said. "Wish me luck."

Alicia and Jake walked to the bucking chute. Jake could see King Minos through the rails. The large bull snorted loudly.

Alicia wrapped more tape around his gloves. "Don't forget," she said, "let your body flow with his." She squeezed his wrists to make sure the tape was tight. Then she handed him his helmet.

Jake carefully hopped over the rail and climbed onto King Minos's back. He tucked his left hand securely under the bull rope and wrapped it tightly.

Jake glanced over to the stands. He could see his family watching him. Dad gave him a thumbs-up.

Jake took a deep breath. Everything slowed down again. The only thing he heard was his own heartbeat thumping in his ears.

When the buzzer sounded, King Minos came out of the gate like a rocket. The bull wheeled into a pinwheel move with a series of high kicks.

With every kick, Jake's brain felt like it was being scrambled in his skull. He gripped the bull rope tighter to stay on.

Then Minos reversed his spin and slammed to a halt. Jake lurched forward against the bull's neck. The bull lifted its rear legs in a powerful kick. Jake's body whipped with the kick. It felt like his head was going to snap off.

Minos tucked into a spin, and everything became a blur again. Jake couldn't tell how much time was left. He just held on with all the strength he had.

When Minos swung out of the spin, he began another series of kicks. Each kick brought them closer to the wall.

With a wild roar and a hard kick, Minos jumped for the wall. Jake flinched. His heart pounded. It would be just like the last time. He squeezed his eyes closed and held on tightly with his left hand.

But they didn't hit the wall. Instead, King Minos swung away in another spiral kicking move.

The buzzer in the arena blared loudly. Jake opened his eyes. Eight seconds had passed.

He'd done it! He'd gone the whole eight seconds on the meanest bull in the division. Letting go of the bull rope, Jake jumped off of King Minos. Then he ran to the side of the arena.

As the rodeo clowns wrangled up the bull, Jake climbed out of the arena and made his way back to his family. He could see his parents and sister on their feet cheering. Alicia and Brandon were hollering too. Up on the scoreboard, his name slid into the tenth-place spot.

Jake grinned. He felt great. Sure, he hadn't placed first, second, or even third. He'd placed tenth. But that didn't matter to him anymore. This tenth place felt better than all his championships.

Jake realized that his dad had been right. He'd needed to cowboy up and overcome his fear. That's what was most important. And he'd done it. That felt better than any first-place trophy.

He reached his family and friends in the stands. Everyone was on their feet cheering loudly.

"Way to go, Jake!" Alicia yelled. "That was amazing!"

"That was awesome, man!" Brandon added. "I can't believe you lasted the full eight seconds!"

Jake leaned over and high-fived Brandon with his good hand. Then he turned to his dad.

"You were right, Dad," Jake said. "I just had to dust off and get back in there. I had to cowboy up."

ABOUT THE AUTHOR

Scott R. Welvaert lives in Chaska, Minnesota, with his wife and two daughters. He has written many children's books, including *The Curse of the Wendigo* and *The Mosquito King*. Most recently, he has written about Helen Keller, the Donner Party, and Thomas Edison. Scott enjoys reading and writing poetry and stories. He also enjoys playing video games and watching the Star Wars movies with his children.

ABOUT THE ILLUSTRATOR

When Sean Tiffany was growing up, he lived on a small island off the coast of Maine. Every day until he graduated from high school, he had to take a boat to get to school! Sean has a pet cactus named Jim.

GLOSSARY

arena (uh-REE-nuh)—a large area that is used for sports or entertainment

chute (SHOOT)—a narrow passage for something to pass through

concentrate (KON-suhn-trate)—to focus your thoughts and attention on something

corridor (KOR-uh-dur)—a long hallway or passage in a building

discouraged (diss-KUR-ijd)—having lost your enthusiasm or confidence

enormous (i-NOR-muhss)—extremely large

ligament (LIG-uh-muhnt)—a tough band of tissue that connects bones

reigning (RAYN-ing)—ruling

tense (TENSS)—nervous or worried

trough (TRAWF)—a long, narrow container from which animals can eat or drink

DISCUSSION QUESTIONS

1. After Jake saw Alicia riding left-handed, he came up with a creative solution to his problem. Talk about some other ways he could have dealt with his injury.

2. What are some other things Jake's friends could have done to help him?

3. What do you think about Jake's attitude throughout the book? Talk about how it changes from beginning to end.

WRITING PROMPTS

1. At the end of this book, Jake rode King Minos for eight seconds. Write about a time when you had to "cowboy up" and overcome your fears.

2. Write about a time you accomplished something you were extremely proud of. Did anyone else help you? How did you do it?

3. Would you ever want to try bull riding? Why or why not? Write about it!

MORE ABOUT BULL RIDING

Bull riding is a rodeo sport that involves a rider attempting to stay on a large bull while the animal tries to buck the rider off. According to American rules, a rider must stay on the bull for eight seconds.

At the start of the ride, the bull is held in a bucking chute. The rider mounts the bull in the bucking chute, signals when he or she is ready, and the chute door is opened. The bull tries to buck the rider off. The rider must hold the bull rope with one hand, and try to shift his or her body weight to stay balanced on the bull.

Riders are judged based on how well they control the bull and how long they can stay on. They are judged for only eight seconds, when the ride officially ends. An adult bull-riding competition usually has four rounds. The rider who earns the most points from all four rounds wins.

SAFETY EQUIPMENT & TIPS

BULL ROPE — the rider hangs onto a braided rope that is tied behind the bull's front legs

CHAPS — provide protection for the rider's legs and thighs

GLOVES — leather gloves to help the rider grip the bull rope and prevent rope burn

HELMET — helmets with ice-hockey-style face masks are mandatory at younger levels

PROTECTIVE VEST — riders are required to wear a protective vest made of high-impact foam

There are several youth organizations that are designed to encourage youngers riders to get involved in the sport. To learn more, check out:

- Texas Youth Bull Riders
- National Junior Bull Riders Association
- Western Regional Bull Riders Association

4 NEW TITLES

JAKE MADDOX

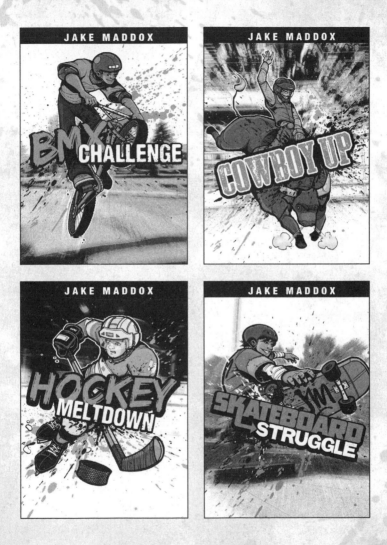